Maka the Magic Music Maker

A Tale From Hawai'i

Story by **Shannon Scott**

Illustrations by **Holly Braffet**

Includes an audio CD with an original song by Domonic Vespoli and a reading by Shannon Scott!

BEACHHOUSE

Long ago, in an old Hawaiian village, lived a shy keiki kāne. His name was Maka.

He didn't talk much, but he loved to sing. And he loved to play his 'ukulele.

Every time he played it and sang his song,
people would stop what they were doing
and sing along.

It was called the "Maka Shaka Shuffle."

Point your thumb,
now point your pinky.
Shake it back and forth
and give a little winky.
It's the Maka Shaka Shuffle,
OH YEAH.
The Maka Shaka Shuffle,
UH HUH.

Point your thumb,
now point your pinky.
Shake it back and forth
and give a little winky.
It's the Maka Shaka Shuffle,
OH YEAH.
The Maka Shaka Shuffle,
UH HUH.

No matter what people were doing—playing 'ulumaika, eating poi, or even fishing, when Maka played his 'ukulele and sang his song, they would stop what they were doing and sing along.

One day, a massive puaʻa entered their village and began thrashing and eating everything in sight.

He even chased the children around and tried to make them his lunch.

Terrified, everyone ran to find a hiding place. Maka hid high in a tree and watched the giant puaʻa destroy everything in his path.

The puaʻa stopped to snort and sniff a big lauhala basket beneath Maka's tree.

He rocked it with his snotty snout. Then with a sniffle and a snuffle, he pushed the basket over and out tumbled Maka's baby sister, Kalei.

The big red eyes of the pua'a locked
on Kalei. Maka knew he had to do
something, and something fast.

He jumped out of the tree and landed
in front of his sister. There he stood,
face-to-face with the huge beast, his
'ukulele in hand.

The pua'a was startled and before he could make a move, Maka began playing his 'ukulele and sang his mele full of mana—the "Maka Shaka Shuffle."

(At first, he wasn't sure if it would work because a pua'a doesn't have a thumb or a pinky. But he had to try something.)

Point your thumb,

now point your pinky.

Shake it back and forth

and give a little winky.

It's the Maka Shaka Shuffle,

OH YEAH.

The Maka Shaka Shuffle,

UH HUH.

The pua'a was mesmerized by the music.

Maka sang it over and over again and slowly led the pua'a away from his sister and away from his village.

Down the path he walked and sang, the pua'a following him and swaying to the music.

That day, Maka saved his little
sister, his family, his friends, and
his village.

Now in Hawaiʻi, whenever someone
leaves, we raise our hand in the air, point
our thumb and point our pinky, and give a
little shaka—
        just like Maka.

Glossary

keiki kāne—boy
pua'a—pig, boar
'ulumaika—an ancient Hawaiian game, similar to bowling, where you roll a round stone between two sticks
mele—song
mana—power, strength

Acknowledgments

Mahalo to our Heavenly Father who has blessed me with a beautiful family and wonderful friends. My Mom and Dad, Sharon and Lawrence "Scotty" Scott. Thank you for all the love and support you've given and continue to give to me, Mandi, and the girls. Sean, Les, and Max, I love and appreciate you guys. To my wonderful in-laws Joe, Shandra, Joy, and Ola, thanks for everything! To the dancers, family, and friends of Na Maka O Pu'uwai Aloha, we are so blessed to have ALL of you in our LIVES! Domonic Vespoli, mahalo for coming through with the song and the 'ukulele playing. #TalentedMan right there. Alan Okami and KoAloha 'Ukulele, mahalo for the opportunities given and the ones to come. Keep spreading the Magic of Music, my bruddah. Cox Media Group (KCCNFM100), mahalo for allowing me to do what I do! Jane and BeachHouse Publishing, thank you for believing. All my aunties, uncles, grandparents, and other family members, knowing that you're always there means the world to me. To my beautiful, caring, supportive, and sweet wife Mandi, thank you for being my inspiration, my soulmate, and my best friend. Always believing in me and pushing me to do bigger and better things. Finally, my two munchkins Tiani and Moanike'ala. You make us proud, you make us laugh, you make us smile, and you fill our hearts with Love and Joy. Daddy writing this book proves that ANYTHING is possible. Dream big, my angels!

For details on Na Maka O Pu'uwai Aloha and a link to KoAloha 'Ukulele, scan the QR code. Mahalo!

—**Shannon Scott**

Maka the Music Maker

Intro (Hook) C, C, C, F, C C, C, C, G, C (2X)

Chorus:
```
C7              F                 C
His name is Maka, the music maker
                D7   G7           C
Let's do the shaka, just like Maka
```

Hook: C, C, C, F, C C, C, C, G, C (2X)

C, Cmaj7, C7

```
F                              C
Stop what you're doing and sing along
      G7                                    C
He's strummin' his 'ukulele to his favorite song
    F                              C
A shy keiki kāne that loves to sing
      D7                         G7
The Maka Shaka Shuffle is his favorite thing
```

Chorus:
```
C7              F                 C
His name is Maka, the music maker
                D7   G7           C
Let's do the shaka, just like Maka
```

Hook: C, C, C, F, C C, C, C, G, C (2X)

-Instrumental

```
C7              F                 C
His name is Maka, the music maker
                D7   G7           C G7
Let's do the shaka, just like Maka
              C   G7          C
just like Maka, just like Maka
```

Hook: C, C, C, F, C C, C, C, G, C (2X)

About the Author

Shannon Scott is Cox Media Group's promotions director and on-air personality for KCCNFM100, and the host of the television show, *Heineken Hot Hawaiian Nights.* Scott is happy husband to Mandi and proud daddy to Tiani and Moanike'ala.

About the Illustrator

A graduate of Moloka'i High School, Holly Braffet has a BFA from Ringling College of Art and Design, and an MLIS from the University of Hawai'i at Mānoa. Her other BeachHouse books include *Kekoa and the Egg Mystery* and *If You Were a Dinosaur in Hawai'i.* She is a librarian in Hāna, where she lives with her family and three fat cats. When she isn't drawing, Holly knits sweaters for her teapots and reads comic books.

· ·

Text copyright © 2012 by Shannon Scott
Illustrations copyright © 2012 by Holly Braffet
"Maka the Music Maker" song copyright © 2012 by Shannon Scott

ISBN-10: 1-933067-49-7
ISBN-13: 978-1-933067-49-0
Library of Congress Control Number: 2012911491

Design by Jane Gillespie
First Printing, October 2012
Second Printing, April 2013

BeachHouse Publishing, LLC
PO Box 5464
Kāne'ohe, Hawai'i 96744
info@beachhousepublishing.com
www.beachhousepublishing.com

Printed in Korea